There's A COW Under My Bed!

By Valerie Sherrard

Illustrated By David Jardine

Tuckamore Books
a Creative Publishers imprint

St. John's, Newfoundland and Labrador
2008

Canada Council   Conseil des Arts
for the Arts   du Canada

Canada

Newfoundland
Labrador

We gratefully acknowledge the financial support of the Canada Council for the Arts,
the Government of Canada through the Book Publishing Industry Development Program (BPIDP),
and the Government of Newfoundland and Labrador through the Department of Tourism, Culture and
Recreation for our publishing program.

Illustrations and book design © 2008, David Jardine

Printed on acid-free paper

Published by
TUCKAMORE BOOKS
an imprint of CREATIVE BOOK PUBLISHING
a Transcontinental Inc. associated company
P.O. Box 1815, Station C
St. John's, Newfoundland and Labrador A1C 5P9

Printed in Canada by:
Transcontinental Inc.

Library and Archives Canada Cataloguing in Publication

Sherrard, Valerie
    There's a cow under my bed! / by Valerie Sherrard ; illustrated by David Jardine.

Interest age level: For ages 5-11.
ISBN 978-1-897174-34-0

    1. Children's poetry, Canadian (English). I. Jardine, David II. Title.

PS8587.H3867T44 2008   jC811'.6   C2008-904388-X

With much love for my awesome nephews:

Bryce Christopher Cunneyworth Russell

Drew Mitchell Cunneyworth Russell

My name is Oscar Ollie Brown
And there are things that make me frown

That irk, annoy and puzzle me
Because - they're things I cannot see!

The first one is especially strange
For cows live on a farm, or range
And yet each night when I'm in bed
One sneaks in here and licks my head!

My mother tells me this is so,
She combs my hair, it's red you know
And every day while combing quick
Mom has to wet the comb and slick...

A spot that's sticking in the air.
She clicks her tongue and says, "Your hair
Has cow licks in it every day.
There now, it's gone, run off and play."

I've checked my closet, and my drawers
I've looked while crawling on all fours
I've searched and sighed and shook my head
It *must* be underneath my bed.

I've all but given up by now
I just can't seem to find this cow!
And still, each night, with fiendish glee
It sticks its big old tongue on me!

But if you think my only woe
Is this bovine, I'll have you know
That other things I cannot see
Are sneaking up and vexing me

Some days I'm trying to be good
Just as my mother says I should
When we're somewhere a boy should sit
And never squirm or move a bit

I tell myself: I *can*, I *will*
Sit quietly, stay calm and still
But though I do my very best
I'm bothered by another pest.

For though I never *mean* to stir
Especially when I've promised her
That I won't move the slightest bit
The urge to squirm around will hit!

And then my mother sighs and frowns
She tilts her head and leans it down
She whispers with her sternest glance
"You must have ants inside your pants."

Well! I can never check right there
You can imagine folks would stare
And by the time I get to peek
They've all escaped, each little sneak.

It's most perplexing, most unfair
To try to sit still in a chair
And you'd have trouble too, perchance
You had these ants inside *your* pants!

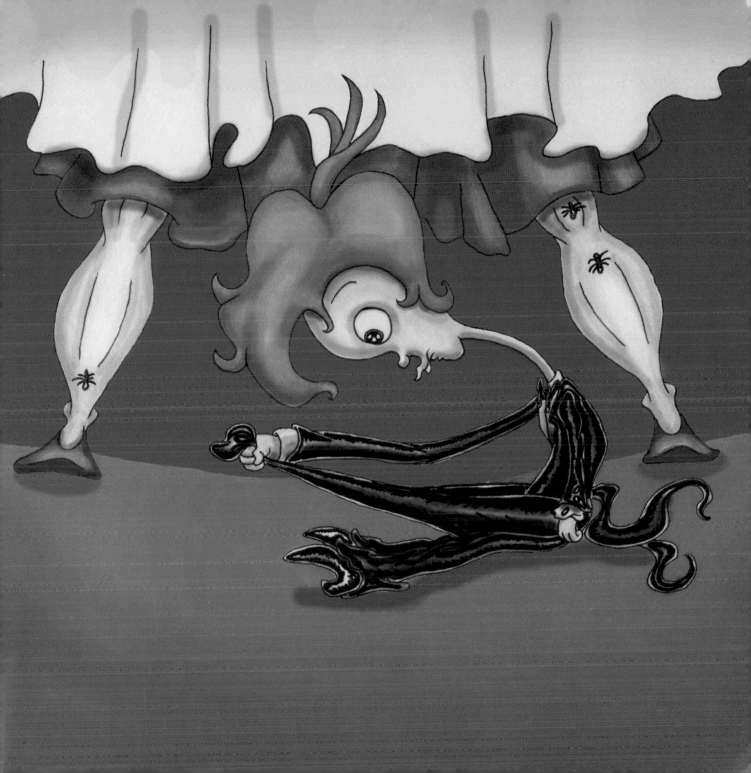

But if you think my problems end
With ants and cows, then think again!
It seems that, though it can't be seen
There's one more creature - cold and green!

I'm telling you, this latest one
Is quite enough to make me run
To flee without my shoes or coat
Because - a frog is in my throat!

It happened just the other day
With something I'd begun to say
Except, when I began to speak
My words were just a creaky squeak.

My mother heard it too, you see
She giggled! Then she said to me
"A frog is in your throat, my lad.
Don't look alarmed - it's not so bad."

Giggle.

It's *not so bad* she dared to say -
While my poor head filled with dismay!
What dreadful news! I felt quite faint
As I checked out this odd complaint.

I found a mirror, looked inside
My mouth was opened big and wide
I stretched till it was big and round
But there was no frog to be found.

Now what's a boy supposed to do
With all these creatures? I'll tell you

There's no escape, no chance at all
When things you can't see come to call.

The ants that won't let me keep still
And cows and frogs - invisible!
But they exist - and this I know
Because my mother tells me so.